ER
DUFRESNE,
M.
5.18 dz

A Bike Ride
FOR JACK

BY MICHÈLE DUFRESNE

CONTENTS

Pioneer Valley Educational Press, Inc.

chapter one
THE BIKES

One morning, Bella
looked out the window.
"Look," she said.
"Dad has the bikes out."

"Oh! I like bike rides.
I hope I get to go!" said Rosie.

"Dad is getting the cart ready.
I think we are going, too!"
said Bella.

"A bike ride!" said Daisy.
"It will be so much fun!"

"Let's go wait by the door," said Bella.
Bella, Rosie, and Daisy
jumped off the bench
and ran to the door.

Jack looked out the window
at the bikes.
"A bike ride?" said Jack.
"I can't ride a bike. I'm too little!"

Jack jumped off the bench
and ran to his pillow.
He sat down.
"I will stay here and take a nap,"
he said.

Daisy looked at Jack.

"Don't worry, Jack.

You don't have to *ride* a bike.

Dad will pull us in a cart.

It will be lots of fun."

"I don't think it will be fun.

I'll stay home," said Jack.

"I like being at home."

"Come on, Jack," said Daisy.

"You will not like being at home.

You'll be here all by yourself."

"OK," said Jack. "I'll go, too.
I don't like staying home
all by myself. But I still
don't think bike riding will be fun."

"You'll see. It *will* be fun!"
said Daisy.

chapter two

THE BIKE RIDE

In the afternoon,
Dad and Mom drove Bella,
Rosie, Jack, and Daisy
to the bike path.

Dad hooked the cart to the bike.
Bella and Rosie jumped into the cart.
Dad picked up Jack and Daisy
and put them into the cart, too.
Then off they went.

Bella looked around.
"This is fun," she said.
"I like bike riding."

"Me, too," said Rosie.

"Me, too," said Daisy.
"This is so much fun!"

"I don't like bike riding," said Jack.
"I want to go home."

"Jack, look!" said Rosie.
"There is a squirrel on the path."

"Where is it?" asked Jack.

"Too late," said Daisy.
"We rode by it."

"Look at the birds," said Bella.
"There are birds in the tree."

"Where are the birds?" asked Jack.

"Too late," said Bella.
"We rode by them."

"I am getting out," said Jack.
"I don't like bike riding.
I want to see the squirrel
and the birds.
We are going too fast."

"Oh, no," said Rosie.
"Jack, no, no, no! Stop!"

Jack jumped out of the cart.

"Oh, no!" said Rosie.

"Oh, no!" said Bella.

"Jack! Jack!" cried Daisy.

Jack looked around.
"Oh, no," he said.
"They left me behind!"

Jack ran down the bike path.
"Wait! Wait for me.
I changed my mind!
I *do* want to go for a bike ride!"

"Maybe I do like
bike rides," said Jack.
"Now I can see everything!"